Just In Case You Ever WONDER

Max Lucado

Illustrated by Toni Goffe

JUST IN CASE YOU EVER WONDER

Managing Editor: **Laura Minchew**

Project Editor: **Brenda Ward**

Library of Congress Cataloging-in-Publication Data

Lucado, Max.
 Just in case you ever wondered / by Max Lucado; illustrated by Toni
Goffe
  p. cm.
 "Word kids!"
 Summary: A parent tells a child how special she is, both to the
parent and to God.
 ISBN 0-84990978-3
 [1. Parent and child—Fiction. 2. Christian life—Fiction.]
I. Goffe, Toni, ill. II. Title.
PZ7.L9684Ju 1992
[E]—dc20
                                                             92-25059
                                                                CIP
                                                                 AC

Printed in the United States of America
2 3 4 5 6 7 8 9 RRD 9 8 7 6 5 4 3 2 1

*Jenna, Andrea, and Sara, this book is
for you—just in case you ever wonder.*

Long, long ago God made a decision—
a very important decision…
one that I'm really glad He made.
He made the decision to make you.

The same hands that made the stars *made you.*
The same hands that made the canyons *made you.*
The same hands that made the trees and
the moon and the sun *made you.*
That's why you are so special. God made you.

He made you in a very special way.

He made your eyes so they would twinkle.

He made your mouth so you could smile.

He made your laugh so you could giggle.

God made you like no one else.

If you looked all over the world—in every city in every
house—there would be no one else like you...

no one with your eyes,

no one with your mouth,

no one with your laugh.

You are very, very special.

And since you are so special, God wanted to put you in just the right home…

where you would be warm when it's cold,

where you'd be safe when you're afraid,

where you'd have fun and learn about heaven.

So, after lots of looking for just the right family, God sent you to me. And I'm so glad He did.

I'll never forget the first time I saw you...

   your eyes were closed,

   your fingers were curled in two little fists,

   your cheeks were puffy and round.

I knew in my heart God had sent someone very wonderful for
me to take care of.

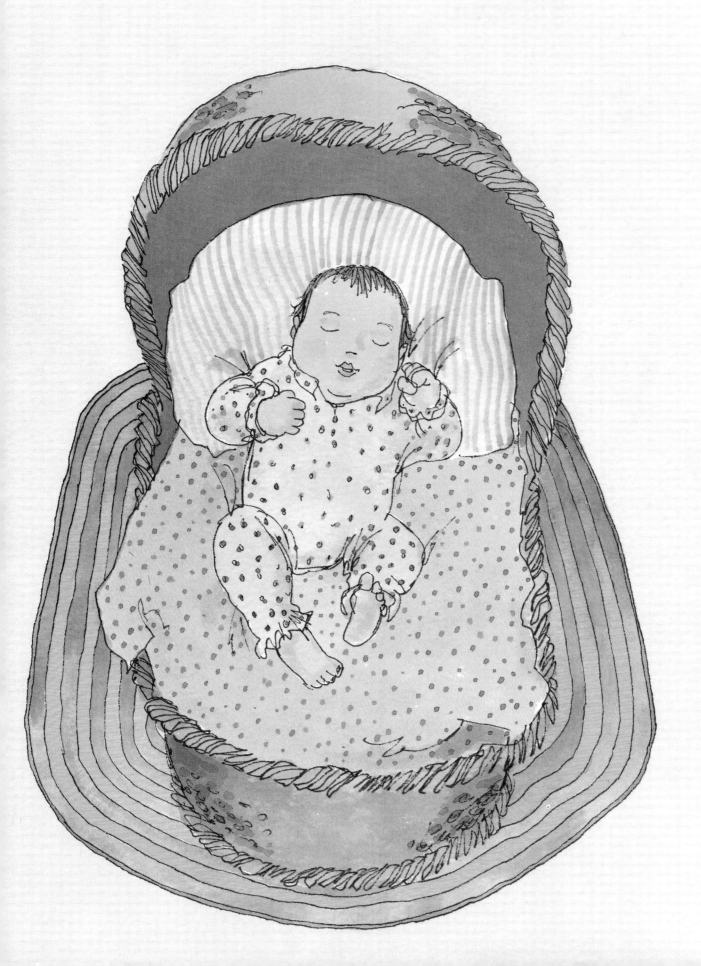

Your first night with me I heard every sound you made:

I heard you gurgle,

I heard you sniff,

I heard your little lips smack.

I heard you cry when you wanted to eat, and I fed you.

You're bigger now and do more things.

You can walk and run.

You can play and talk.

You can eat and sing and look at books.

You're not a little baby any more.

But as you grow and change, some things will stay the same.

I'll always love you.

I'll always hug you.

I'll always be on your side.

And I want you to know that...just in case you ever wonder.

Remember I'm here for you.
On dark nights when you hear noises in your closet,
call me.

When you see monsters in the shadows, call me.

On hard days when kids are mean and don't treat you like they should, come to me.

If your grades are bad and your teacher is mad,
come to me...'cause I love you.
And I always will, just in case you ever wonder.

Most of all, I'll be here to teach you about God.

He loves you.

He protects you.

He and His angels are always watching over you.

And God wants me to make sure you know about heaven.

It's a wonderful place.

There are no tears there.

No monsters.

No mean people.

You never have to say "good-bye,"
or "good night,"
or "I'm hungry."
You never get cold or sick or afraid.

In heaven you are so close to God that He will hug you, just like I hug you. It's going to be wonderful. I will be there, too. I promise. We will be there together, forever. Remember that...

just in case you ever wonder.